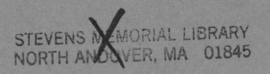

Emma & Mommy Talk to God

Marianne Williamson

—— and ——

Emma Williamson

Illustrated by Julia Noonan

HarperCollins*Publishers*

Library of Congress Cataloging-in-Publication Data
Williamson, Marianne, date
    Emma & Mommy talk to God / by Marianne Williamson and Emma Williamson;
illustrated by Julia Noonan.
        p.   cm.
    Summary: Because Mommy teaches Emma that God is present in everyone in the
world, Emma learns not to be afraid and even asks God to help Peter.
    ISBN 0-06-026464-0.
    [1. God—Fiction.]   I. Williamson, Emma.   II. Noonan, Julia, ill.   III. Title.
PZ7.W6725Em   1996   95-1697
[E]—dc20   CIP
                                                                                                 AC

1   2   3   4   5   6   7   8   9   10
❖
First Edition

For Norma Ferrara,

who is one of our angels

—M.W.

For Hope

—J.N.

Every morning, Emma and Mommy talk to God.

"Thank you, God" is what they say.

"Thank you for the flowers. Thank you for the trees.

Thank you for the rain. Thank you for the sky."

One morning when Emma
was getting dressed,
she asked Mommy,
"Where do I come from, Mommy?"
"From God, sweetheart,"
said her mother.
"God loves you very much,
and he loves Mommy too,
so he sent you to Mommy
so we could be together."

"Mommy," said Emma,

"who is God?"

"God is all the love

in the world,"

said Mommy.

"He's in you and in me

and in everybody

everywhere."

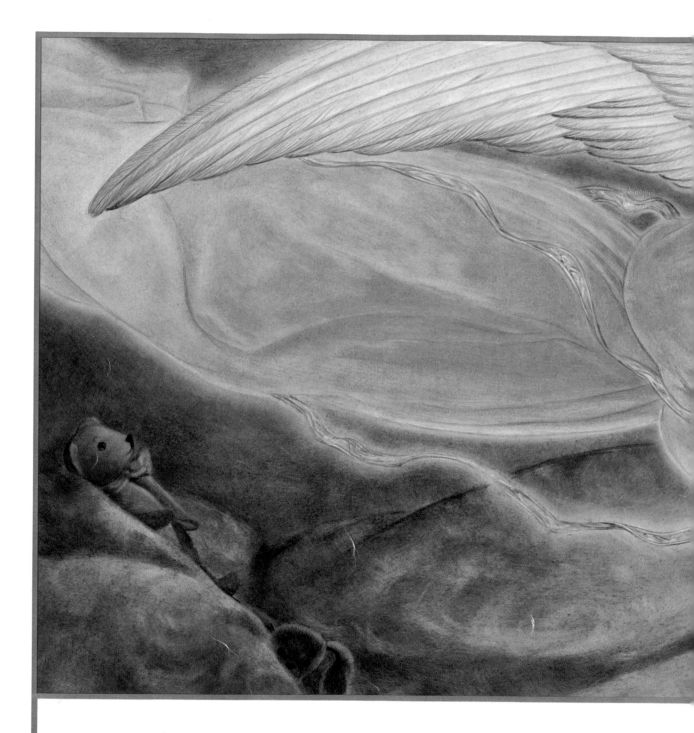

That night, Emma had a dream about an angel.

The angel said, "Emma, God has sent you to earth.

He is always with you. He is in your heart.

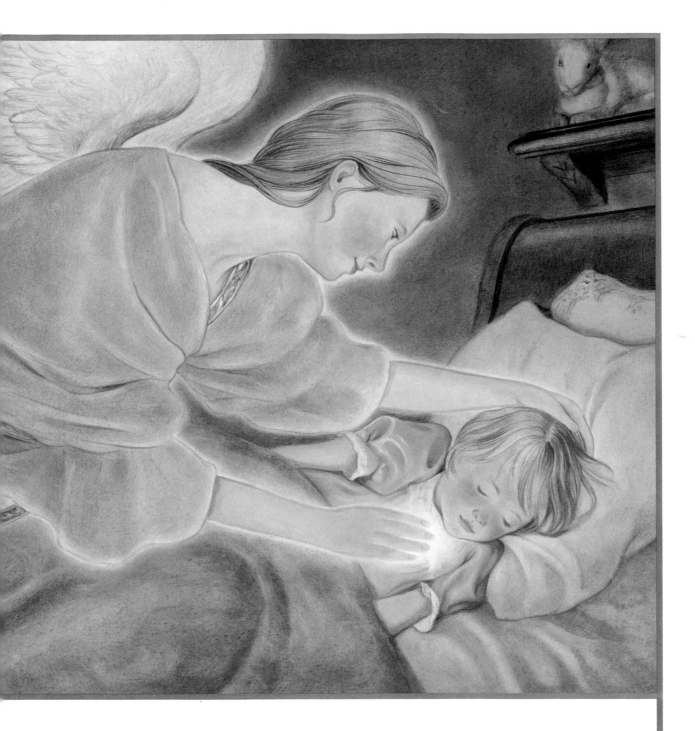

He will always be there to take care of you and tell
you what to do whenever you have a question."

The next morning, Emma asked Mommy
what the angel had meant.

Mommy said, "The angel was telling you
to trust God, Emma. God is always with us.

Every day, tell God how you feel.

God always hears you and sees you, darling.

Whenever you need anything,

just ask God for help.

Every day tell Him

how much you love Him.

That's what it means to pray to God."

Then one dark night,

Emma woke up.

She was all alone in her room

and she was very scared.

She started to cry.

And then she remembered

what Mommy had told her.

Emma remembered

that she was never alone

because God is always with her.

As soon as she remembered that, she felt
love surround her like a soft, fuzzy blanket.

She knew the angels were in her room.

She stopped feeling sad and started feeling happy.

Soon after that,
Emma told Mommy
about a little boy
at school.
The little boy had
been mean to Emma.
He had thrown sand at her.

"Mommy," said Emma, "is God in Peter too?

Why was he so mean to me?"

"Yes," said Mommy, "God is in Peter too.

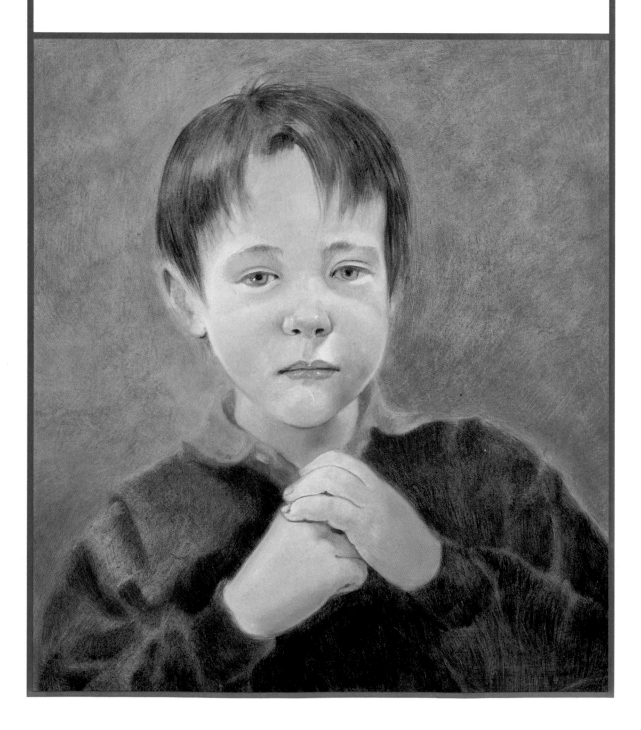

But deep in his heart Peter is very sad and scared.

Pray for Peter, Emma,

and ask God to make him happy."

So Emma prayed for Peter.

She asked God to send the angels
to him and make him very happy.

The very next day, Emma dropped her sweater.

Peter picked it up nicely and gave it back to her.

Emma knew in her heart that God had helped Peter.

After school,

Emma told Mommy

about Peter and the sweater.

Mommy was glad and said,

"I'm proud of you, Emma.

You did the right thing.

You're a wonderful little girl.

I love you."

Emma said,

"Thank you, Mommy.

I love you, too."

She felt very happy.

And then she added, "Thank you, God."

Dear Friends,

I believe that the most urgent need of parents today is to instill in our children a moral vision: what does it mean to be a good person, an excellent neighbor, a compassionate heart? What does it mean to say that God exists, that He loves us and He cares for us? What does it mean to love and forgive each other? Parents and caregivers of children must play a primary role in returning our society to a healthy sense of the sacred. We must commit to feeding our children's souls in the same way we commit to feeding their bodies.

Parents are the primary spiritual teachers of our children. We hold them in our arms and whisper in their ears before the world has the chance to bruise their tender spirits. I think there is no greater gift we can give our children than the knowledge that there is a God, a supreme, all-loving, all-merciful Being, who is there for them every moment of their lives. And there is no greater gift that we can give to God than to teach our children well of His forgiveness and His love.

I hope that *Emma & Mommy Talk to God* is a support for parents as well as children. We have no more important job to do than to remind the generations that follow us of the existence of God's power, and of how, through prayer and forgiveness, we can experience His love in our daily lives. Such is the revolution of faith, which will, I believe, heal our hearts and heal this world.

Sincerely,

Marianne Williamson
Emma's Mommy

July 1996

jp
Williamson, Marianne

Emma & Mommy talk to God.